ALDYWNS

Dear Young Seeker of Magic,

Let me be the first to welcome you to the world of wizardry! As an outstanding young candidate for the study of magic, you have received this book to prepare you for your upcoming studies at Aldwyns Academy for Wizardry.

Aldwyns Academy for Wizardry is the premier school for the study of magic for talented girls and boys. We retain a first-class facility with extensive alchemical gardens, nearly ten thousand books on the magical world and theories of spellcraft, and the best professors teaching in the world of wizardry today.

During your time at Aldwyns, we will provide for your room and board. You must arrive at school with a few supplies, but don't worry—the following pages will let you know what you need and guide you through the entire process. A complete list of required books will be provided to you after you have registered for classes.

Study this book well. For as surely as the practice of magic is filled with wonder and delight, it is also filled with danger and perilous adventure. It is the well-educated wizard who survives to tell stories of both.

That's "good travel"   —— Fawel Sevef,
to the unstudied!   Archmage Lowadar
                                      Headmaster, Aldwyns Academy

A Practical Guide to

WIZARDRY

Compiled by

Archmage Lowadar

Headmaster, Aldwyns Academy

MIRRORSTONE™

At Aldwyas, first-year students wear red robes. After the first year, the color of your robes indicates what type of magic you practice.

You will need at least three everyday robes and one ceremonial robe for special occasions. You will also need at least one pair of boots, one belt with pouches, and a wand.

Snap holster for quick release.

Pouches to hold spell components. A wizard can never have enough pouches, but for the thrifty wizard (or student, like you), three will suffice.

Wizards can't wear more than one ring per hand. The magic of rings is so potent that having more than one in such close proximity can interfere with the magic of both rings.

Magic symbols on boots often tell the maker and the spells infused in the boots.

WIZARDRY ESSENTIALS

Preparation separates good wizards from great wizards. Great wizards always carry the supplies they need to remain ready for whatever challenges they may face—whether taming a wild dragon or embarking on their first year at Aldwyns Academy.

A Wizard's Wardrobe

Without their signature wardrobes, wizards look just like everybody else. So wizards developed the habit of wearing a hat and robes to announce their status. During your stay at Aldwyns, you will be expected to keep up the tradition. Luckily for you, there are now a variety of stores that cater to the clothing needs of a wizard. You are sure to be able to find something to suit your taste.

The color of a wizard's robes corresponds to the type of magic he or she specializes in.

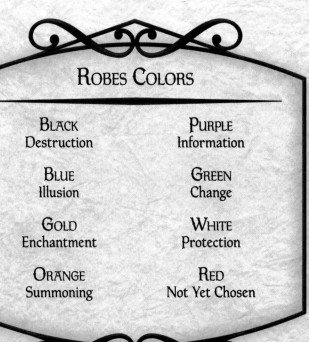

ROBES COLORS

BLACK Destruction	**PURPLE** Information
BLUE Illusion	**GREEN** Change
GOLD Enchantment	**WHITE** Protection
ORANGE Summoning	**RED** Not Yet Chosen

When you're packing for Aldwyns, you'll want to make sure you stop in the town outside the academy and pick up some of the following parts of a basic magical wardrobe. Let them know it's your first year at Aldwyns, and you're sure to get a special new-student discount!

Footwear

A wizard's footwear is more than just something to cover the feet. Boots often contain enchantments that allow the wizard to do such things as cross lava (like Dragonscale Boots) or leap across a lake (like Seven League Boots). A proper wizard has a closet full of boots—a different pair for each occasion. First-year students should arrive at Aldwyns with—at minimum—Slippers of Spider Climbing to scale the tower where classes in information magic are held and Boots of Speed for everyday use.

Boots of Speed are necessary because classes are sometimes very far apart, and there is not much time between classes. Students need to be able to move quickly. Careful not to run into anyone!

Hats

Tall and pointy, or floppy and wide-brimmed, a wizard's hat serves many purposes. It is everything from a place to stash a snack to a hiding place for a familiar. A hat can also carry enchantments that allow the wearer to speak languages not known otherwise or to take on someone else's appearance. Aldwyns students are not required to wear hats. But you should plan on purchasing a Hat of Reduce Size for illusion class.

Taught by a pixie in a classroom sized for pixies!

Belt

A wizard's belt is essential. While rarely enchanted, a wizard's belt often has a carrying case for his wand as well as attached pouches containing spell components. Wizards who expect trouble often have a holster for their wand. The wand snaps onto it, and easily snaps off if its owner needs to cast a spell in a hurry. Students will want to make sure they pack a Belt of Spell Resistance among their gear. First-year wizards' spells have a tendency to backfire, and such a belt will provide students with a little extra protection should their magic go awry.

A Wizard's Wand

Wands are the instruments through which wizards cast their spells, focusing and shaping magic. Without a proper wand, your magic is greatly weakened and more likely to fail. A good wand, on the other hand, will make your spell effects more accurate, reliable, and powerful. Take the time to have a wand selected specially for you, at least for your first wand. That way, if you ever need to buy a replacement wand, you will know what to look for.

Some wizards use orbs or staffs in place of wands. At Aldwyns, all students are required to learn wandwork before proceeding on to other instruments.

The shape the carvings take express the wizard's personality.

Shaft

The shaft forms the connection between the wand and the wizard. It can be made from wood, bone, crystal, or metal. While you can choose any material for your wand, it is usually best if you choose a shaft according to the season of your birth.

Spring birthday: Living wood
Summer birthday: Crystal
Autumn birthday: Bone
Winter birthday: Metal

Carvings

A wand's carvings reflect the spirit of the wand and its wizard. After you select the shaft the wandsmith creates the magical carvings.

Focus

A focus concentrates the arcane energies collected in the wand. Any crystal used as a focus must be flawless! If there is a flaw in the crystal, the spells you cast with it will backfire.

Charms

Charms make the spells a wizard casts in a particular area stronger. If you like casting fire spells, you might want to get phoenix feathers for your wand. Or if you tend to cast summoning spells, try dragon teeth.

FOCUS CHOICES

QUARTZ
A pure, unclouded crystal of quartz is hard to come by–a rare but perfect find if you want to study information magic.

FIRE OPAL
Red as flames and just as temperamental, a fire opal nearly doubles the power of any fire spell cast through it. If you like destruction magic, choose a fire opal.

AMETHYST
The favored gem of faeries. You might want to consider amethyst if you're interested in enchantment magic.

MOONSTONE
Bits of moonlight caught and given form, a moonstone is the perfect choice if you are drawn to illusion magic.

TIGEREYE
Shaped like the eyes of the beasts you'll summon, a tigereye has an affinity for summoning magic.

PEARL
A pearl–once mere dust, but transformed into a gem through years in an oyster–is the natural choice if you're interested in change magic.

JADE
Normally cool to the touch, this green stone turns burning hot when danger is near, making it the best focus if you want to specialize in protection magic.

Magic Items

In addition to casting spells, wizards sometimes enchant items with magic. Not all items can be enchanted— only the highest quality objects can hold magic without being destroyed. There are an endless variety of magic items. We've listed a few here that we recommend you acquire.

Goggles of Minute Seeing are particularly useful as many of our spellbooks and tomes were written by way of magic, and are thus inscribed in a far smaller text than the human eye can see.

Goggles of Minute Seeing

Through these goggles, the lines on your fingertips look as deep as hedge mazes, and pixies seem as large as giants. Gold-rimmed and carved from glass, these goggles will allow you to read even the tinest writing.

Heward's Handy Haversack

Heward's Handy Haversack is almost essential to your stay at Aldwyns. The bag is about the size and shape of a normal backpack, but it will hold all of your schoolbooks and equipment without weighing a pound more than it did when you first put it on.

Phoenix Cloak

A phoenix cloak is made out of the finest gold mesh, inlaid with rubies and covered with delicate gold feathers. Yet it feels as light and as soft as silk. What is more, whenever you wear a phoenix cloak, you have only to wish to fly, and the cloak will carry you wherever you wish to go, with the speed and the skill of one born to fly. Though not required, a phoenix cloak is recommended for all students who plan on taking summoning courses on magical creatures, as a number of the creatures we study are aerial in nature, and are best observed in their home environment.

Ring of Bright Eveningstar

A Ring of Bright Eveningstar is a carved platinum ring set with a large brilliant stone (usually a diamond) nestled among a collection of other gems. All glow brightly in even the deepest darkness. On the inside of the ring is an engraving in Elvish. When wearing a Ring of Bright Eveningstar, you can summon light with a whispered magic word whenever you wish, making this hands-free alternative to torches the perfect ring for nocturnal alchemy classes. Without this ring, collecting ingredients that bloom only at night can be difficult indeed!

Usually sapphires and rubies

Alchemy 201: Night-Brewed Potions

Slippers of Spider Climbing

These soft, silken slippers allow you to walk up walls and across ceilings as easily as you walk across the floor. They are required gear for your classes in detection, scrying, and communication spells—which take place at the top of Aldwyns' Tower of Information Magic. The Slippers of Spider Climbing also add an exciting element to otherwise mundane games.

Scrying allows you to see what others are doing through magical means.

Map of Unseen Lands

This map is based on the legendary map of the halflings, and has many of the same properties. The map appears blank when you unfurl it, but then, as you watch, the map draws itself in. The map is always a perfect rendition of the immediate area, including the homes of any magical creatures nearby. Unlike the legendary map of the halflings, the map doesn't cover very much area, and can be used only once a day. But it is very useful for students looking to find spell components or trying to pick their way through dangerous territory.

Wand Bracelet

One of the most useful items you can purchase for Aldwyns is a wand bracelet. This small golden chain is enchanted to shrink one of your normal-sized items into a charm that you can attach to the bracelet. The wand bracelet can hold up to four items—a perfect way to keep your wand, your spellbook, a pouch of spell components, and an emergency lunch with you at all times.

Weapon charms will be confiscated just the same as weapons!

Scarab of Aradros

While amulets are banned at Aldwyns, a Scarab of Aradros is awarded to the school president at the beginning of the year as a mark of their station and reclaimed at the end of the year for the next school president. The Scarab of Aradros is more than ornamentation— it improves your ability to counter spells and resist spell effects. It can also prove an adorable pet, growing warm when paired with a talented student and chirping occasionally.

School president is determined by the dueling tournament at the Grand Wizardry Games!

Other Suggested Magic Items

Goggles of Night

Pearl of the Sirines

Bracelet of Animal Friendship

Glove of Storing

Crystal Ball

Can be purchased in the mail room

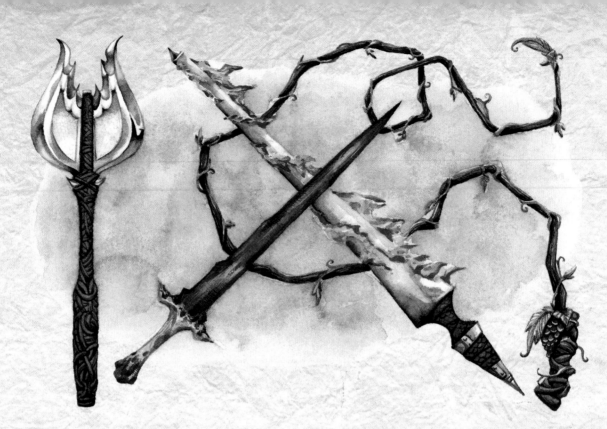

Banned Magic Items

Not all magic items are welcome at Aldwyns. Some magic items are dangerous or disruptive to class, and are banned on school property. If you are caught with any of the following items, the magic item will be confiscated, and you will be assigned to one of the less pleasant jobs at Aldwyns for a week (such as mucking out the pegasi stables or weeding the snapping dragon gardens).

Weapons

Your goal at Aldwyns is to learn, and weapons do not make for a safe learning environment! Still, some students persist in bringing their uncle's Blazing Skylance or their brother's Crystal Echoblade. And then before you know it, one student or another gets to spend the next week or so regrowing all their hair. At Aldwyns, all weapons are confiscated on sight.

At the Award Ceremony of the Grand Wizardry Games, glitter stones are allowed as part of the festivities.

Additional Forbidden Items

Portable Holes	Ring of Invisibility
Glitter Stones	Dust of Sneezing and Choking
Sovereign Glue	
Eversmoking Bottle	Necklace of Endless Laughter
Drums of Panic	Elixir of Fire Breath
Universal Solvent	Pipes of the Sewers
Girdle of Change Gender	Rope of Entanglement
Ring of X-Ray Vision	Elixir of Love

Amulets

Amulets are a traditional part of the wizard's wardrobe, but while at Aldwyns, students are prohibited from wearing them. While you are at Aldwyns, we expect to educate and test the knowledge and skills you have learned through hard work and studying, not that which you have acquired through coin spent on intelligence- or skill-boosting amulets. Amulets that provide students with magical tricks, like the Amulet of Second Chances, are likewise prohibited, though for very different reasons. These amulets are often dangerous and rarely find their way into student hands by accident.

Amulet of Second Chances: When this hourglass is flipped, the world goes back in time. Time-play is outlawed not only at Aldwyns, but in the world of wizardry as a whole.

Cursed Items

These magic items often appear like normal magic items, but do terrible and unexpected things to wizards who try to use them. What is worse, many of the effects of these cursed items can be hard to reverse, so what may start out as a practical joke may leave its victims in the Health Room, undergoing a time-consuming de-cursifying process.

Cursed Raptor's Mask: Bought by a young first-year student off a lone traveler last year, this mask makes the bearer dance uncontrollably. It took Professor Ives's sternest spells to remove the cursed item.

A Wizard's Familiar

Wizards' lives are full of change, but one thing stays the same: they always have their familiars by their side. A familiar is an animal who acts like a pet for a wizard—only a familiar is much more than a pet. It has a deep connection with its wizard and can help with tasks from the mundane to the magical.

At the beginning of the school year, all first-year students without familiars are invited to participate in the Festival of Choosing. This is a weeklong event during which students learn how to call a familiar, then gather the materials necessary for the summoning spell, and await their familiar's arrival. A familiar may come as quickly as after a few minutes, or it could take as long as a week! At the end of the week there is a party celebrating all the wizards with their newfound familiars, with special treats for the familiars.

Very rarely, a dragon familiar chooses a wizard. If this happens to you, you must report to Professor Dunbar to receive special training in working with your dragon familiar.

Last year, a boy named Claude had a most unfortunate experience at the Festival of Choosing. He got hungry before the festival was over and ate the food that was supposed to be for his familiar. As a result, his familiar was a pig!

Calling a Familiar

When a wizard calls a familiar, it is actually the familiar that chooses the wizard. The wizard has no idea what kind of animal will appear. The only thing for certain is that the animal is the perfect match for the wizard.

Sometimes, though, a familiar has already chosen its wizard, even before the festival begins. In this case, the familiar is just waiting for the wizard to participate so that their already strong connection can be bound with magic. You can usually tell if an animal has chosen you if it seems like the animal understands you.

No Room for Mistakes

Once the calling process begins, the wizard cannot eat, drink, speak, or move until a familiar has come and accepted the wizard's offering. This can take hours, or even days to finish. If you participate in the Festival of Choosing, it's important that you follow the directions to the letter. If you make a mistake, your familiar will not come, and you will have to wait a year before you can try again.

Find Your Familiar

What familiar will choose you? Take this quiz before the Festival of Choosing to help you anticipate which animal will be your lifelong magical companion.

1. You have a quiz in information magic today, but you forgot to study. You:

   a. know the answers anyway—school is easy!

   b. answer the questions as well as you can.

   c. copy a friend's quiz.

   d. decide you don't like information magic anyway.

   e. ask the teacher if you can take the test another time.

2. You find a bag of magic pebbles that turn into candies when you put them in your mouth. You:

   a. turn the bag in to lost and found.

   b. bring it back to your room and share the pebbles with your friends.

   c. try to make candy that turns into pebbles when you put it in your mouth.

   d. decide to keep it—it's good candy!

   e. didn't "find" the bag so much as convince someone to give it to you.

3. You accidentally bump into another student on the way to class and books are spilled everywhere! You:

   a. recognize your favorite book and tell the student how much you liked it.

   b. stop and help the student pick up the books.

   c. would never be so clumsy.

   d. catch all the books before they hit the ground.

   e. glare at the student for getting in your way.

4. While the teacher's back is turned, another student pushes you down! You:

   a. run and tell a teacher.

   b. ignore the other student.

   c. hide.

   d. push the other student back.

   e. tell the other student you want an apology—and you get one!

5. You are forbidden from going into the Dark Forest, but one of your friends is lost in there! You:

   a. tell a teacher and ask for help.

   b. get some friends and go in after your friend.

   c. sneak in alone—you've always wanted to see the dark forest!

   d. are lost in the forest with your friend—you never let an adventure pass you by!

   e. convinced your friend to go in there in the first place.

6. You find a box with a carving of a skull on the top, with a warning not to open it. It is locked. You:

   a. notice a secret panel on the bottom that holds a key.

   b. tell your friends about the box to see if they know anything about it.

   c. pick the lock and open the box—you have to know what's in that box!

   d. shoot a magical missile at it from afar to blast it open.

   e. get someone else to open it for you.

Results

Mostly As:
It doesn't take an oracle to figure out that you're likely to get an owl! An owl is an expert at seeing things others miss. While an owl's wisdom and keen sight are useful for any wizard, its skills are particularly well suited to a student of information magic. So if you see information magic in your future, you may want to hope for an owl!

Mostly Bs:
That hungry look in my familiar's eye says you're likely to get a rat! But don't worry—even my familiar knows that a rat is the most dependable and stubborn of friends, and is much more useful alive than serving as a dragon's snack. A rat is a resourceful ally for any wizard. But in particular, the heart of a student who enjoys protection magic has a special place for a rat's tenacity and strength. So if you're looking to use magic to help others, hope for a rat!

Mostly Cs:
You're purrrfectly suited for a cat! A cat is a master of subtlety and sleight of paw. It is a rare wizard who doesn't wish to have a cat's stealth and speed upon occasion, but an illusionist tends to put a feline friend to the best use. So if you like to play and illusions are your favorite game, you may want to hope for a cat!

Mostly Ds:
Your fiery temperament is a match for a dragon! A magical creature in its own right, a hatchling dragon often bonds with a wizard to learn more about magic. A dragon's allure is hard for any wizard to deny, but a student of destruction magic has the most to learn from a dragon's natural talent for magic. So if you like playing with fire, I'd hope for a dragon!

Mostly Es:
I've a sneaking suspicion you'll get a snake! The most charming and persuasive of familiars, a snake slips right into a wizard's heart. A snake's charismatic nature makes it particularly helpful to an enchanter, so if you want to study enchantment, hope for a snake!

A Wizard's Bond

When a familiar chooses a wizard, a lifelong magical connection is formed. This bond is so deep that a wizard can actually understand what the familiar is saying—and be understood in turn by the familiar. This communication is not verbal, but rather mind to mind. They can even communicate in this manner over a great distance, which makes a wizard and a familiar the perfect team.

Over time, you and your familiar will become more and more alike, sharing mannerisms and even quirks of appearance. A wizard with a cat familiar may develop catlike eyes, an affinity for cleanliness, and a habit of curling up in pools of sunlight. Likewise, the familiar may take on the wizard's love of books, its face may begin to resemble the wizard's, and it may lounge in positions remarkably similar to that of the wizard. Your familiar will also be strengthened by its bond with you, becoming more resilient and intelligent. It will live as long as you do.

A magical way of talking that is possible only because of the strength of the bond between them

A love of books is often expressed by curling up on them.

You can tell a lot about a wizard by looking at the familiar.

Familiar Care

Caring for your familiar is different than caring for your average pet. For one thing, a familiar requires a great deal more attention. To maintain your bond with your familiar, you should spend at least one hour a day doing an activity that your familiar enjoys. This can be playing a game, sunning yourselves side by side, going on a long walk or swim, or whatever your familiar desires. Your familiar will let you know other needs as they arise. Remember: a happy familiar is a helpful familiar.

INSIDE ALDWYNS

Aldwyns is an extensive facility, and it takes time to get used to all its twists and turns. The map on the following page should help you find your way to your classes. Be sure to give yourself extra time to get to your classes your first week or so! There is a five-minute grace period for the first week, but after that, you will be counted tardy if you are not in your seat by the time a class starts.

Life at Aldwyns is not all study and no play—on certain occasions, students may receive permission to explore the magical town surrounding Aldwyns. Most of the town's residents are former students of the academy, and all of them are wizards. The town is a place where wizards can exchange magical lore, locate or create enchanted items, or even just talk to a few fellow wizards. Remember, you are free to buy whatever you wish in town, but whatever you take back with you to Aldwyns is subject to our banned magic-items list.

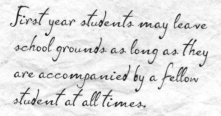

First year students may leave school grounds as long as they are accompanied by a fellow student at all times.

LOST AND FOUND

If you ever get lost and need help finding your way, just point your wand at the ground and shout *"Aldwyns enmur fawel upwo,"* followed by the name of the place you are trying to go, and blue magic will blossom on the ground and light the way there. Be warned: this only works on school property. Once you leave school grounds, you are on your own!

Tower of
Change Magic

Tower of
Summoning Magic

Tower of
Illusion Magic

Tower of
Destruction Magic

Tower of
Protection Magic

Tower of
Enchantment

Tower of
Information Magic

Aldwyns Academy for Wizardry

Aldwyns Academy for Wizardry

1. Entrance

2. Statue of School Mascot, Daelicasus the Dragon (currently made out of chocolate due to a school prank)

3. Grand Ballroom: Filled with glittering magical lights, and tiled in polished moonstone, this shimmering chamber is where the awards ceremony for the Grand Wizardry Games is held, as well as the graduation ball. The ember red tiles that make up the stylized "A" on the floor are rare dragonsbreath rubies, a priceless gift from the crystal dragons at the laying of the foundation of this school.

4. Dining Hall: Our food has been rated among the best of all the world of wizardry, thanks largely to our head chef, Pebin Nowells. Meals are at sunrise, midday, and sunset. Be sure not to be late, as the dining hall is only open for an hour for each meal!

5. Mail Room

6. Study Hall (Spellcraft Theory and Spellwriting classes held here)

7. Headmaster's Quarters: These are my personal quarters. Should you ever have a need for me, don't be intimidated by the heavy blackrock door, magical wards, or the fancy titles.

8. Health Room

9. Third- and Fourth-Year Dorms

10. Vault of Wondrous Things: Whether a professor needs a magic item for a demonstration, or a student needs one for a class, this is where all the school's enchanted equipment is kept.

11. Closet of Confiscated Magic Items: No matter how many times we warn students, they still bring banned magic items in to school.

12. First- and Second-Year Dorms

13. Athadora "Bones" Darkspell's Old Chambers (Closed!): Students say strange noises and smells still waft from her chambers at night.

14. Enchanted Cupboard of Spell Components

15. Library

16. Information Magic Observatory: You'll need Slippers of Spider Climbing to reach the top of this Observatory. From here, you can see the colors and movements of the stars in a way that makes a nonmagical telescope seem crude in comparison.

17. Old Whiskers' the Dragon's Favorite Roost: Whiskers, the current dragon patron of the school, enjoys resting here, so it is a good place to scout around for shed dragonscales. You can hear his snoring even from the far towers!

18. Flying Carpet Picnics here on weekends.

19. Watch your step! Elemental Spells class practices summoning ice here.

20. Summoning Chambers: Buffeted by extra protection spells, roomy enough to summon larger creatures, and bound within strong stone walls, this is the perfect place for students to try out their new Summoning spells.

21. Ever-Changing Hedge Maze

22. Alchemical Gardens

23. Pixie Passages (old forgotten service tunnels into the depths of Aldwyns)

24. Magical market held here weekends. (Good place to buy rare spell components!)

25. Theater of Illusion: If you've never been to an illusionist-run theater, you're in for a treat! In this theater, with the help of talented illusion students, dragons roar and breathe fire, oceans sweep over the stage in one scene to be replaced with castles in the next, and music, smells, and sensations sweep over the audience.

26. Watch out! Infestation of imps here

27. Destruction Magic Firing Range

28. Ultimate Flying Disc played here.

Student Dormitory

When you get to Aldwyns, you will be assigned to a dormitory where you will live with another student, known as your Magical Guide, who will help you adjust to life at the school. Your Magical Guide will be a second-year student studying the type of magic you are most interested in. First-year students study all the types of wizardry, but after you complete your first year of wizardry training, you must pick a type of magic to concentrate your studies in. Your Magical Guide can give you a taste of what school would be like if you picked their chosen specialty, as well as helping you with your homework and adapting to life at Aldwyns.

Remember, while you can change what type of magic you'd like to concentrate on at any time during your first two years, your Magical Guide is your partner for the whole first year.

Most of the first- and second-year student dorm rooms overlook the Alchemical Gardens.

Use ring gates for retrieving forgotten homework

Homunculus

Magic glowstones light most of the desks.

HOMUNCULUS

Flying around like a doughy, misshapen faerie, a homunculus is a harmless extension of a wizard's will. You can take a class in homunculus creation at any point during your time at Aldwyns, and the result is one of these sweet but ugly little friends.
A combination of your magic and enchanted clay, they reflect your personality almost exactly, and can serve as messengers, note-takers, and friendly paperweights. A homunculus also makes a good guardian, as its bite can send an attacker into a harmless slumber that allows you to get out and find help.

Second-year students get the top bunk

All desks have a cleaning enchantment on them to keep your homework neat and your spell components from mixing.

Window

Ring Gate

Light on Desk

Beds

Desk

Bed for Familiar

Cage for Familiar

Student Dormitory

A familiar often sleeps during the day while its wizard is in class.

A wizard's familiar would never try to leave its wizard, but sometimes it's good to have a home that provides a little extra protection—particularly if your roommate's familiar looks hungry!

The Library

You will find a great deal of your time at Aldwyns is spent right here in the school's library: studying, reading up for classes, or looking up answers for the Great Treasure Hunt. We have an extensive collection of rare tomes from all over the magical world, ranging from High Wizard Zendric's treatise on the different kinds of monsters, to Sindri Suncatcher's *A Practical Guide to Dragons*. If you ever need a book not contained in our shelves, ask the librarian, and she will send an enchanted letter to one of our sister schools to see if they have it in their collection.

We do ask that you take care not to scare the books in the back section of the library during your stay. They have been acting up lately and fly about at the least provocation, their spellbindings notwithstanding. It takes the poor librarian hours to herd all the books back onto the shelves where they belong.

See Grand Wizardry Games

A pixie named Pollena

Aside from a general section for use by first-year students, the books in Aldwyn's library are shelved in accordance with the Nibeloneus Number System. If you need help locating a book that you seek, you may either consult Pollena or refer to the magical catalog (requires special training!). Requests for specific book titles may also be submitted from the comfort of your student dormitory via ring gate.

Watch out!
Some books bite!

Aldwyns Alchemical Gardens

Nymph's Glen: With her skill at healing and her soothing enchantments, Kaelie the nymph is one of the primary caretakers of Aldwyns Alchemical Gardens.

Old Whiskers the Dragon's Cave: A good place to collect shed dragon scales for spell components.

Cavern of the Quivering Mushrooms: If you make too much noise here, the mushrooms will start quivering, dropping enough spores to send you to sleep for a week.

Pixies' Nest: Illusion classes taught here by Professor Keene.

Snapping Dragon Gardens: Watch your fingers! Students are required to wear dragonhide gloves when pruning the snapping dragon plants.

Ever-Changing Maze: The enchanted plants in this maze move into new designs every day. If you ever get lost, chant *Seero Vee'ex Sevef*, rub a leaf over the tip of your wand, and point it ahead of you to make a path through all the plants in your way.

Reflection Pool: Always take a buddy when swimming in the Reflection Pool. The waters are deeper than they appear, and host a variety of waterlife.

Dryad's Grove: Under the tender care of Professor Witchhazel, some of the trees in the Dryad's Grove have lived for over a century. No axes or fire are allowed in the Dryad's Grove.

Spider's Crawl: The spiders here are huge! But we feed them well, so they are quite friendly.

In addition, some of our more unusual professors make their home in the garden.

Aldwyns Alchemical Gardens

Courses in alchemy are recommended throughout your stay at Aldwyns, and all first-year students take Introduction to Alchemy during their first semester at school. Quite a few alchemy classes take place in the heart of this useful garden, and homework for the class often entails gathering ingredients for various potions.

Many of Aldwyns' recreational activities take place in the Alchemical Gardens. From swimming in the Reflection Pool to caving and rock climbing near the Cavern of the Quivering Mushrooms to watching firemoths in the Snapping Dragon Gardens at night, there is always something fun for the adventurous student to do. In addition, many clues in the Great Treasure Hunt are designed to help students explore the strange and wondrous sights hidden in the depths of the gardens.

While the gardens are as safe as we can make them, nature—and magic—always carries an element of danger. So be prepared. Keep your wand and spell components handy, and treat the gardens and garden residents with the utmost care and respect.

The Mail Room

Most wizards at Aldwyns communicate using enchanted letters, which fly around as thick as faeries at a midsummer dance, particularly around the holidays. If you are in need of a more immediate form of communication, the mail room can accommodate most students' needs.

The following items can all be purchased or rented at any time during the school year.

Rings of Communication

These rings are perfect gifts for your friends. Though they only work within a short distance, once they are attuned to each other, the bearers of these rings can talk to each other whenever they want to, no matter where they are or how loud the circumstances.

Ring Gates

This pair of iron rings, connected by magic, is perfect for the student studying away from home. Anything put through one ring ends up in the other ring. You can even reach through one ring and grab items that are close by the other. Whether you need a fast way to pass messages, or need to consult your library at home, the ring gates are quicker than a homunculus, and less expensive than a portal.

Crystal Balls

With a simple spell, these orbs of pure crystal can allow you to see and speak to anyone you wish—though the person you are communicating with will need a crystal ball themselves if they wish to see you as well. Crystal balls are a great way to keep in touch with your family and friends back home without ever having to leave the school. Crystal balls are expensive, so while you are welcome to purchase your own crystal ball, we have several available in the mail room for students' use only.

Portals

At first glance, these human-sized stone circles appear to be nothing more than decoration. Yet with the proper magic words, blue runes appear and begin to glow on the stones of the circle. The air between the stones begins to swirl and takes on the image of the place you designated. All you have to do is step through the circle, and you will find yourself exactly in the location shown by the portal. They are perfect for emergency trips home, or for field trips, where large groups of students will be going to the same location. Be warned, though: these are one-way portals. You will need to find your own way back to school at the conclusion of your trip.

Portals are located on the back wall of the mail room.

Ring Gates

Professor Keene
Head of Illusion Magic

Professor Witchhazel
Head of Enchantment Magic
& Alchemy

Professor Fife
Head of Information
Magic & Spellwriting

Professor Ives
Head of Protection Magic

Professor Grimsby
Head of Change Magic
& Spellcraft Theory

Professor Blackburn
Head of Destruction Magic

Professor Dunbar
Head of Summoning Magic

TYPES OF WIZARDRY

In change magic, for instance, you can choose to study transformation, movement spells, or enhancement spells—very different fields united under the study of change magic.

Your advisor will be one of the wizards pictured on this page

All first-year students at Aldwyns must take introductory courses in alchemy, spellwriting, and spellcraft theory, as well as at least one course in each of the seven types of wizardry. Each specialty of magic encompasses a wide variety of spells, so there are often several introductory classes from which to choose.

The following pages will provide you with information about each of the courses offered to first-year students. Remember: these courses form the foundation of your study at Aldwyns. Some of the courses you have the option to take are prerequisites for higher-level courses you may want to take in the future. So study this book well. Once you arrive at Aldwyns you will meet with your advisor, who will help you craft your schedule for the year.

General Classes

All first-year students must take the following classes:

- ☑ Alchemy 101
- ☑ Spellwriting 101
- ☑ Spellcraft Theory 101

Elective Classes

Please select one class from each of the following types of wizardry:

Destruction Magic
- ☐ 101: Elemental Spells

Illusion Magic
- ☐ 101: Lights and Sounds
- ☐ 102: Invisibility

Enchantment Magic
- ☐ 101: Curses
- ☐ 102: Love Spells

Summoning Magic
- ☐ 101: Animal Friends
- ☐ 102: Teleportation

Information Magic
- ☐ 101: Detection Spells
- ☐ 102: Scrying
- ☐ 103: Communication Spells

Change Magic
- ☐ 101: Transformation
- ☐ 102: Movement Spells
- ☐ 103: Enhancement Spells

Protection Magic
- ☐ 101: Shields and Wards
- ☐ 102: Counterspells

Destruction Magic

All wizards should study the art of combat for self-defense as well as to help keep the wizarding world safe from monsters and dark wizards. Destruction magic is the wizard's answer to swords and fists. It is an art that involves harnessing the power of the elements. Legend has it that long ago, wizards made a pact with the spirits of fire, earth, air, and water. This pact granted the wizards who follow the path of destruction magic fantastic power, but also tremendous responsibility. Destruction magic is far from subtle and is an example of the perilous forces that wizards can learn to command.

You may use dandelions or other weeds as targets for practicing Magic Missile—the destruction wizard's first and often favorite spell!

The job of a wizard specializing in destruction magic is to seek out and destroy evil. As such, the students who make the best destruction magic wizards tend to be passionate, proud, and brave. Most of the students who study destruction magic have a temper, and so part of a destruction magic wizard's training is learning to keep a firm grasp on emotions and allow reason to rule the use of magic.

Destruction magic is the most dangerous of the wizardly arts. If a destruction magic spell goes awry, the results are often devastating—turning the effect of the spell back on the caster! Therefore, it is very important to study hard, make sure you get each syllable of every spell correct, and use exactly the right amount of every spell component. Destruction magic is not for the lazy or faint of heart.

In more formal wizarding circles, destruction magic is known as evocation.

Magic Missile

Magic Words: ᛉ ꙮ ꝯ

Wand Signs: Draw a small circle counterclockwise in the air with your wand, raise your wand to the sky, then point the tip of your wand at the target.

Spell Components: None

SAMPLE SS SPELL

Sample Destruction Spell

Magic Missile. This classic destruction magic spell is beloved in part because it requires no spell components, and in part because it never misses its target—when performed correctly. A correctly cast Magic Missile is a vivid green color and shoots out from the tip of your wand with a sound like bacon sizzling. If the target moves, the Magic Missile veers to follow, and if the spell hits, it explodes on the target in a shower of green sparks.

Courses in Destruction Magic

Destruction Magic 101: Elemental Spells. When lightning strikes, do you think, "How exciting!" rather than cower under your bed? If you answered yes, then you have a lot to look forward to. In Elemental Spells, you will learn how to tame the elements and use them as your sword. Fire will blossom, lightning will strike, ice will pelt, and stone will rain down on your command. A large portion of this class will be devoted to the proper use of this dangerous form of magic, and all students must pass a test on the ethics of destruction magic before they can enroll in the subject's more advanced courses.

This course is a prerequisite for all other courses in destruction magic, including Destruction Magic 201: Fireballs, Destruction Magic 202: Elemental Storms, and Destruction Magic 302: Sonic Combat.

Illusion Magic

Picked up from the playful sprites of the dark forest, illusion magic is the wizard's art of deception and misdirection. Often playful and persuasive, wizards who practice illusion magic work to convince their audience—be it an attacking troll or a classroom full of young wizards—that the illusions they create are real. Due to the performance aspects of illusion magic, students who excel at this art tend to have persuasive, charming, and creative personalities.

Illusionists are the wizarding world's entertainers and some of the best teachers. Nothing helps a lesson in history pass quickly like watching what actually happened, instead of reading a book full of facts with no color or sound.

Theater of Illusion

For students interested in acting or helping with special effects, we have a theater club at the school. Every year, two plays are put on in Aldwyns' Theater of Illusion. Our next winter play is *Secret of the Spiritkeeper.* Augmented with a combination of student alchemy and illusion, the plays are always impressive to behold. All students are welcome, but students skilled in illusion are particularly in demand.

*A skilled student of illusion
can create a magical double that
does everything they do.*

Playing with a person's mind is always dangerous, but never more so than when you're dealing with illusion magic. Illusion magic is lies given form and substance—undetectable and untraceable when done well. The opportunities for abuse are many, as outlined by the Laws of Ethical Wizardry, from convincing one friend of another's betrayal, to making a pit seem like solid ground.

Wizards who practice illusion magic must learn restraint above all else, for once you slip down the path of using illusions to fool people and get your way, you will not only lose friends, honor, and integrity, you will also lose sight of yourself.

Courses in Illusion Magic

Illusion Magic 101: Lights and Sounds. Seeing is believing, right? In Lights and Sounds, you will learn how to make people see and hear things that aren't really there—and so believe in whatever you wish them to believe in. This class makes a great companion course with alchemy.

Illusion Magic 102: Invisibility. Just as in Lights and Sounds, where you learn to make people see and hear things that aren't there, in Invisibility, you learn to make things people can see and hear unseen and silent. You will learn spells to make all kinds of things invisible—from yourself, to your familiar, to the writing in a book.

Sample Illusion Spell

Silent Image. This is illusion magic at its most pure: it creates a silent, moving picture that you control. You'll be asked to make an image of your favorite animal so that the class can see your skill at illusion. One of the things that makes this spell a favorite is that the spell component for it is minimal, and it does not get consumed in the spell, so only needs to be bought once.

Most students choose their familiars so they have something to base the illusion magic on!

This is a classic illusion magic spell!

Silent Image
SAMPLE SPELL

Magic Words: ꧁ 𐤟 ⵊ ꓔ

Wand Signs: Draw the outline of the creature you want to create in the air with your wand, raise your wand to the sky, and point the wand at where you want the Silent Image to appear.

Spell Components: A bit of fleece. Rub the fleece on your wand before casting the spell.

Masters of enchantment can always count on dryads for companionship and conversation when they adventure abroad.

Enchantment Magic

Little did we know, when the dryads of the forest first came and taught us the art of enchantment magic, how dangerous this mild, subtle art could be! Enchantment magic is the art of twisting the hearts and minds of others to your will. When used for good, enchantment magic is among the most gentle of the wizardly arts; but when used for evil, it is the most insidious, for it can turn the best of friends into deadly enemies. All students are required to study at least a basic level of enchantment.

Because of the delicate nature of the art, students with a knack for enchantment magic tend to be empathetic, insightful, and strong of heart. It takes a rare kind of student to specialize in enchantments. But that student's natural talents, once augmented with enchantment magic, make them peerless diplomats and mediators.

Enchantment magic is easily abused. A wizard who specializes in this art must always keep the subject of the spell in mind. Just because you want someone to like you doesn't mean you should cast a spell to make that person like you. Enchantment spells are not permanent in any event. After the spell wears off, the subject will remember that they had been charmed, and they may not look too kindly upon you for that.

A student who can read the minds and emotions of others, and know when to use their art and when they should not makes the best enchanter.

Sleep
SAMPLE SS SPELL

Magic Words: 𐤊 𐤌 𐤓

Wand Signs: Draw a circle in the air in a clockwise direction with the tip of your wand, circling the number of times equal to the number of minutes you want the subject to be asleep, then point your wand at whomever you want to fall asleep.

Spell Components: Fine black sand, the last petals of a rose's wilting bloom, and a live cricket. Rub the rose petals on your wand before casting your spell, blow the black sand on your subject during the spell, and kiss the live cricket after finishing your spell.

Sample Enchantment Spell

Sleep. This spell can stop a fight before it even begins. It is the best defense in any combat situation, and a great cure for insomnia. Casting Sleep is time consuming, however, since for every minute you want the subject to sleep, you must circle your wand once.

This spell—one of the first you will learn—is a perfect example as to why enchantment magic is required study for all students!

Courses in Enchantment Magic

Enchantment Magic 101: Curses. Also known as "revenge magic," curses are the wizard's retort to bullies and monsters. In Curses, you will learn how to cast spells that will daze opponents, cause them to laugh or dance without being able to stop, or make them as dull-witted as an ogre. You will also learn how to use curses responsibly.

Enchantment Magic 102: Love Spells. More dangerous than any curse is love magic. In Love Spells, you will learn to cast a spell that will charm a troll into falling in love with you. You'll also learn how to put a classmate to sleep with a magical lullaby, and how to make an enemy wizard treat your suggestions as if they were advice from a trusted friend.

Summoning Magic

Passed down for generations among small families of desert wizards, summoning magic is the art of magically calling animals and other creatures to help you, as well as the art of teleportation.

Summoners are among the most adaptable and useful of wizards, making excellent explorers, scouts, and guardians. Need to retrieve something from high in the treetops? This art will allow you to summon the right creature for the job. Students who become successful summoners tend to be willful, driven, and meticulous.

Spells of summoning must be cast with incredible precision. Should even one line be out of place in the summoning circle you draw, or one word mispronounced, then at best the creature you summon will not appear—and at worst, it could attack you. Always make sure to have a summoning partner around when you attempt a summoning spell so that you have help in case something goes awry.

Another student or the teacher

The oldest magical traditions call summoning magic conjuration.

When you summon your familiar during the Festival of Choosing, you will be casting your first summoning spell!

The bigger the animal, the harder it is to summon!

Courses in Summoning Magic

Summoning Magic 101: Animal Friends. No wizard adept at summoning magic is ever really alone. Animal Friends teaches you to summon animal friends: otters, bears, dogs, eagles, spiders, cats—whatever you wish! Animal Friends is a prerequisite course for Summoning Magic 201: Magical Friends, in which you learn to summon dragons, unicorns, griffons, and other magical creatures.

Summoning Magic 102: Teleportation. Summoning magic is not just magically moving creatures from somewhere else to where you are—summoning magic is also magically moving things from where you are to somewhere else. And that place can be almost anywhere, depending on your skills at teleportation magic. In Teleportation, you will learn to return your spellbooks to your room, to send your familiar across the class, and to teleport yourself to the dining hall for lunch—all with just flicks of your wand.

Professor Dunbar always says: "Use caution when summoning spiders!"

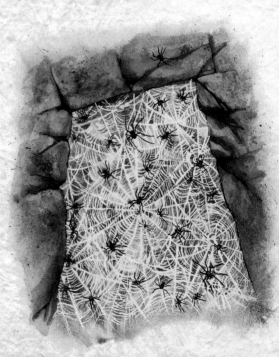

Sample Summoning Spell

Summon Monster. Although the spell is called Summon Monster, the first magical creatures you'll be able to summon are mostly animals like dogs, spiders, and cats. This allows you to practice without serious side effects should you make a mistake in casting the spell. And though these summoned animals aren't the most powerful of beings, they can be very helpful in any number of tasks, from carrying messages to helping defend you should you need it.

My favorite animal to summon is this one.

Summon Monster

Magic Words: 𝄢𝄐𝄑𝄒

Wand Signs: Draw a circle in the air the size of the creature you want to summon with your wand, raise your wand to the sky, and point the wand at where you want the summoned creature to appear.

Spell Components: A tiny bag and a small candle. Light the small candle and dip the tip of your wand into the tiny bag before casting your spell.

SAMPLE SS SPELL

Information Magic

What does this magic cloak do? I wonder where my familiar is? How can I talk to this dragon? Information magic answers all these questions and more. While all wizards use information magic, it is used most extensively by the detectives of the wizarding world, who use information spells to solve mysteries and prevent crimes.

Almost every wizard can learn information spells, but it takes more than good spellcraft to make use of information magic. The wording of your spell is also important, because if you ask the wrong question, the answers will not help you solve your problem.

For instance, if you cast a spell to find out which of your classmates stole your lunch, your spell will fail if your lunch was eaten by your familiar!

If you want to specialize in information magic, you will learn things you did not necessarily want to know—about yourself, your friends, and the world around you. And there will be those who would like to stop you from discovering the truth. To study information magic you must be able to keep secrets as well as root them out, and know when it is better if the knowledge you found stays hidden.

Many wizards who practice information magic prefer to call it divination.

That way, you don't have to figure it out the hard way!

Courses in Information Magic

Information Magic 101: Detection Spells. The simplest, but perhaps the most useful of all information magic, Detection Spells teaches you how to cast a spell to learn an object's magical properties, how to tell if there are secret doors or invisible creatures nearby, and how to see magical auras. This class is recommended for all students interested in the study of ancient ruins or unknown magic items.

Information Magic 102: Scrying. In Scrying, you will learn how to use fortune-telling cards, a crystal ball, and magical fire to see what is going on with other people and places while you are not around. This class is a prerequisite for both Information Magic 201: Scrying the Future, and Information Magic 202: Scrying the Past.

Information Magic 103: Communication Spells. In Communication Spells, you not only learn how to cast a spell that allows you to understand and speak other languages, you also learn how to read people's thoughts and how to let them read yours. This is invaluable for times when you need to communicate but can't risk being overheard, or for when you want to talk with wizards from far away places.

The use of Communication Spells during testing is considered cheating!

You may only use the magical fire in Professor Fife's classroom with supervision.

Identify

Magic Words: ᔕ◍ᒪᴇ

Wand Signs: Draw a clockwise circle over the object you wish to identify with your wand, then tap the object you wish to identify.

SAMPLE SS SPELL

Spell Components: A pearl, an owl feather, and kraken oil. Powder the pearl with your mortar and pestle, pour the kraken oil into the powdered pearl, and stir the whole mix with the owl feather. Dip your wand in the mixture and draw a circle under each of your eyes, and one in the middle of your forehead.

Sample Information Spell

Identify. Whenever you find a magic item and you don't know what it does, Identify allows you to figure out its properties. You will know *before* you put the magic ring you found on whether it will allow you to fly or turn you into a toad.

Cards

Cards are the first objects through which you will learn to cast information spells. By casting a spell and laying out these cards, you will learn the answers to your questions. Each of these special cards has a picture on it with two meanings—one if the card is facing the right direction, another if it's reversed. When you lay the cards out, you place them facedown in a specific pattern, where each position is a different part of your question. You flip the cards over and try to puzzle out what the answers to your questions are by looking at what cards ended up in which positions.

Crystal Balls

One of the other techniques you will learn involves a crystal ball. You cast the information spell and wait for images to rise to the surface of the cloudy sphere, giving you your answers. These images are often mysterious and symbolic, but are sometimes very literal as well. For instance, if you want to know what someone is doing at that very moment, you can use a crystal ball to scry on them.

Fire

Advanced students will learn to cast information spells using fire. To divine using fire, you gather incense, throw it into a fire, ask a question, and cast a divinatory spell. The spell will cause you to answer your own question, aloud, in the form of a riddle.

Remember—you may only cast these spells on school grounds

Change Magic

Before there were wizards, people dreaming of riches tried to figure out how to turn lead into gold. In change magic, focusing on the wizard's art of transformation, you will actually learn the spell for this age-old task—and the ethical reasons as to why you should never use it.

As dreamers who can see possibility in dreary reality, students with an aptitude for change magic tend to be artistic, decisive, and intelligent. A specialist of change magic must have incredible belief in their decisions if they are to impose their designs upon reality.

As change magic is so central to spellcraft theory, the wizards who specialize in it often become professors or magical theorists. However, due to their versatility, they can fill almost any position in society they wish to.

Change magic gives you the power to turn horses into mice. It is a powerful gift that can, with one spell, transform a creature's entire existence. No one wants to pursue a rogue master of change magic, for they don't know if they'll be spending the rest of their days as pigs, or if when they knock on the door of the rogue wizard's tower, they'll be facing a dragon instead of a mere wizard.

Some wizards prefer to call the art of change magic transmutation.

Note: This course only covers transforming willing creatures. Turning your ex-best friend into a pig will have to wait!

Courses in Change Magic

Change Magic 101: Transformation. In Transformation, you will learn how to cast a spell to shrink a classmate down to the size of a pixie—or enlarge them to the size of a giant! You will also learn spells to turn yourself or others into frogs, elves, or even trees.

Change Magic 102: Movement Spells. In Movement Spells, you will learn how to move things without touching them, how to move through walls, and how to fly. No wizard should be without a firm basis in Movement Spells, but it pairs especially well with destruction magic.

Change Magic 103: Enhancements. In Enhancements, you will learn spells to make you and your friends smarter, faster, stronger, and more skilled. You will learn spells that allow you to climb walls like a spider, breathe underwater like a fish, and see in the dark like an owl.

The High Wizard Tamora once said, "Change magic is the art of changing the appearance of things to reflect the way they are inside." She was fourteen and speaking of her ex-best friend, whom she had just transformed into a pig. (Her teacher returned him to his natural shape, but the lesson holds true to this day.)

Sample Change Spell

Reduce Person. Whether you are heading to Enchantment class in the Pixies' Nest or gathering glow-fungus in the crawl spaces of the Cavern of the Quivering Mushrooms, Reduce Person is the perfect spell for wizards with big ambitions in small places. You can also use Reduce Person to cut an opponent down to size. Even the most powerful wizards aren't nearly so imposing when they only come up to your knees.

One of my favorite change spells!

Reduce Person

Magic Words: ⟲Ж⁂

Wand Signs: Draw a circle in the air, starting with the wand tip at the height of the person you want to shrink and ending with the tip at the height you want that person to be. Point your wand at the person you would like to shrink (even if that person is you)!

Spell Components: A pinch of powdered iron. Sprinkle the iron in a circle around you before you cast the spell.

SAMPLE SS SPELL

Protection Magic

From the moment the first fireball was cast, there has been a call for protection magic. Protection magic is wizardry's art of defense—protection against dark wizards and their equally dark magic. Protection magic is required for first- and second-year students, and it is recommended throughout your career at Aldwyns.

Defenders of the defenseless, and fearless in the opposition of evil, students who excel in protection magic tend to be brave, selfless, and quick-witted. Experts at the counterstrike, these wizards can get inside their opponents' heads and figure out how dark wizards will strike before they themselves know. As well as being good defenders of the wizarding world, wizards who practice protection magic also make good arbitrators for duels.

Protection magic is not a coward's art, for these wizards see more danger in a week than most wizards see in a year. When faced with their worst fear, a protection magic wizard must be able to look it in the eye as they work to counter it. When a wizard turns outlaw, a protection magic wizard is sent to take them in. When danger is about to strike and all other wizards are fleeing, wizards who practice protection magic rush to the heart of the conflict.

See Wizardry Duels

Wizards who study this art exclusively call it abjuration.

Courses in Protection Magic

Protection Magic 101: Shields and Wards. The key to a good magical defense is preparation—and that's what this class is all about. In Shields and Wards, you will learn to craft magical shields that will protect you from even the most powerful spells. You'll also learn how to set magical wards to warn you if someone's sneaking up on you, so that you can be ready to surprise them instead!

Protection Magic 102: Counterspells. Once engaged in combat with an enemy wizard, you'll find that all the preparation in the world can only do so much. Evil wizards are notoriously creative, and will find a way around your wards and shields. That is why it is good to study counterspells! In Counterspells, you will learn to cast spells that cause an enemy's spells to fail, backfire, or reflect back on them.

Counterspells is a requirement for all students interested in competing in the Grand Wizardry Games.

You will not know what shape your shield spell will take on until your first attempt at casting it.

Shield

Magic Words: ΨＯＧ

Wand Signs: Draw a clockwise circle in the air in front of you, then touch the tip of your wand to your heart.

Spell Components: None

SAMPLE SS SPELL

Sample Protection Spell

Shield. This is the wizard's first defense—perfect because it requires no spell components and so can be cast quickly and without much preparation. When you cast Shield, you summon an invisible field of energy that floats in front of you and protects you from harm.

Shield even makes sure that Magic Missile, the spell that never misses, hits the shield instead of you! When a Magic Missile hits a Shield spell, just for a second, the invisible shield is illuminated in electric green light. The shape of a wizard's shield spell, revealed this way, is often very telling as to personality of its caster. A sneaky wizard's shield spell, for instance, might be a snake, whereas a brave wizard's shield spell might be a wolf.

The most important protection magic spell you will ever learn.

Death Magic

Death magic is the dark art of creating, raising, and controlling the dead. Wizards who specialize in death magic work with unholy abominations, enslaving the dead who dearly deserve their rest, and draining the lives of the living before they've gone to the grave.

The practice of death magic is banned at Aldwyns, and throughout the world of wizardry, by the Laws for Ethical Wizardry. Anyone found practicing death magic will be given one warning, and then expelled.

Old spellbooks sometimes reference death magic as necromancy.

Athadora Darkspell taught alchemy at Aldwyns until Professor Fife discovered an altar hidden within her quarters. Before the wizarding authorities could be contacted, Athadora fled. Students are urged to stay far away from any wizard practicing death magic. If you witness anything suspicious, you must report it immediately.

WANTED

NAME:

Athadora "Bones" Darkspell

LAST SEEN:

In the Dark Forest next to Aldwyns

WANTED FOR:

Abduction of students, practice
of death magic

Practical Wizardry

In addition to your schoolwork in the specialties of magic, Aldwyns will educate you in all manners of practical wizardry, including alchemy, spellcraft, and wandwork. Before arriving at school, you ought to study the following basics.

Including the reading, writing, and speaking of runes.

Alchemy

In alchemy, you will learn to mix potions with as many magical effects as there are spells in your spellbook. Mixing a potion is just like writing a spell, only instead of runes, you have ingredients. You mix these ingredients together in order to achieve certain magical effects. Potions provide a way for a wizard to cast a spell in advance of needing it so that in the heat of the moment, all you need do is drink the potion to get the desired effects. Unlike scrolls, potions can be used by even a non-wizard. Because it is such an important part of wizardry, all students are required to take alchemy during their first year at Aldwyns.

It is very important when you drink a potion to drink all of it—drinking only part of a potion can have drastic and unexpected side effects.

An alembic is used to distill potions (or their components) to their purest essence. Usually this is done by placing the substance to be distilled in one of the glass vessels (also called a retort), and then lighting a fire under it. This causes the water to boil out of the substance in the primary retort, and go up the tube as steam to collect in the secondary retort. What is left in the primary retort is the pure essence of the original substance.

Alchemy requires precision above all else—potions are like recipes and call for precise amounts of each ingredient. The amount for each ingredient is most often given in weight.

Secondary Retort

Primary Retort

Alembic

Glass Bowl

Glass Funnel

Scale

Mortar and Pestle

A mortar and pestle are required for grinding potion components. You put the spell components in the mortar and use the pestle to grind them up.

The touch of metal spoils magic potions, and clay is porous, so you will want to have a glass bowl and stirring stick to mix potions with.

When pouring the potion from a bowl into a bottle, it is useful to have a funnel so that you don't spill the contents.

Potion Making

Potion ingredients all have several magical properties. These properties, however, are only expressed when used in combination with another ingredient that shares the same magical property. For example, pegasus sweat has the magical property of *fly*. If you drink it raw, nothing will happen. But mix it with quivering mushrooms, recite the proper spell, and before you know it, you'll be soaring among the stars.

It is very important to pay attention to all the properties of your ingredients. *Any* shared property of the ingredients in the potion will be expressed—even ones that you don't want! Besides *fly*, pegasus sweat has the properties *clumsy* and *dizzy*. If you want to make a potion that allows you to fly, find an ingredient with the property *fly* but without the properties *clumsy* and *dizzy*. Otherwise you'll be flying *and* bumping into all kinds of things!

Never use substitute ingredients—not using exactly the proper ingredient can have horrifying results. Such potions are completely unpredictable and are often dangerous both to mix and to drink.

Potions do not take on their magical properties until you recite the spell words.

See the next page for a list of ingredients.

Anything on the top shelf of
the Enchanted Cupboard of Spell
Components is for professor use only.

Cataloging Your Potions

Potions all tend to look similar—and
you don't want to have to taste them to
tell which is which! Use runes to write
the name of the potion. For now paper
and ink will do, but in Alchemy 301
you will learn to magically engrave
the name of the spell directly on the
potion bottle. In addition to labels,
which can be removed from a potion,
a wise wizard uses dyes to help tell
different potions apart. Most potions
have a disgusting flavor. Adding a
little lemon or chocolate sometimes
helps the potions go down. Flavor
can also help identify your potions.

One student substituted dog hair for satyr
fur in a potion once. He grew a tail, and his
hands turned into paws so that he couldn't
even try to fix it! Even after Professor
Grimsby had changed him back, he smelled
like wet dog for a week!

Remember: Always gather ingredients in an ethical manner, and buy from reputable alchemy stores. It is not only cruel to kill animals for their parts, it is against the Laws of Ethical Wizardry. Often you can gather what is necessary from a creature's habitat, and you can even trade with some creatures for what you would like.

Here are some samples of potions you may learn in your first weeks at Aldwyns. Do not make an attempt to mix any potions outside of Professor Grimsby's supervision.

How would you make a potion that allows you to fly? Study the list carefully, write down your answer, and bring it to the first day of class.

SEE IN THE DARK POTION

THREE EYELASHES FROM A BEHOLDER

ONE GRIFFON EGGSHELL—CRUSHED

Mix ingredients in just enough almond oil to make a paste. Add apple vinegar until the mixture is about the consistency of watery pudding. Wave your wand over the potion to draw an eye in the air, and say *seero fawel poclin*. Stir the potion with your wand and down it quickly.

TALK TO ANIMALS POTION

FOUR DRYAD'S TREE LEAVES—GROUND

SNIPPET OF NYMPH'S HAIR

Mix ingredients in equal parts oil and water. Wave your wand over the potion to draw a paw in the air, and say *ahnqua fawel twozee*. Shake the potion up and down quickly, and use it before the oil and water separate.

You will use this potion in Magical Animal Relations 301

Potion Ingredients
(continued)

LEAVES FROM A DRYAD'S TREE:
Talk with animals, uncontrollable dancing, invisibility

DRAGON SCALES:
Shield, numb, strength

EYELASH FROM A BEHOLDER:
Reduce size, turn into a pig, see in the dark

GRIFFON EGGSHELL, CRUSHED:
Fly, dizzy, see in the dark — *crush it using your mortar and pestle*

IMP SPIT:
Reduce size, turn into a pig, clumsy

KRAKEN TENTACLE: — *that's a giant squid*
Breathe underwater, slow, strength

MERFOLK SCALE:
Breathe underwater, sick, shield

NYMPH'S HAIR:
Talk with animals, uncontrollable laughter, inspire love

PEGASUS SWEAT:
Fly, clumsy, dizzy

PHOENIX FEATHER:
Inspire love, sleep, invisibility

PIXIE DUST:
Invisibility, uncontrollable dancing, sleep

QUIVERING MUSHROOMS:
Fly, sleep, reduce size

SATYR'S FUR:
Inspire love, sleep, uncontrollable laughter

TROLL'S BLOOD, CONCENTRATED: — *concentrate troll's blood with your alembic.*
Shield, numb, sick

VAMPIRE TEETH, POWDERED:
See in the dark, dizzy, turn into a pig

WEREWOLF CLAWS:
Talk with animals, uncontrollable laughter, uncontrollable dancing

YUAN-TI TEARS:
Breathe underwater, sick, slow

ZOMBIE FLESH, BOILED:
Strength, slow, numb

Wizard Words

You will find the following words essential to your studies of wizardry.

APPRENTICE: That's what you are! Apprentices are young humanoids like you, learning their first spells. Never underestimate an apprentice, though. We all started as apprentices, and some of the most brilliant minds of the next generation might be lurking beneath school robes.

ARBITRATOR: Arbitrators are the judges of wizardry duels. Usually powerful practitioners of protection or destruction magic, they make sure that duels are safe, clean, and fair.

ARCHMAGE: After a number of years as a high wizard, a few exceptionally talented wizards are promoted to archmage. There are only seven archmages at a time. An archmage is the head of an academy of wizardry, and helps spread magic wherever young potential wizards are found.

FAMILIAR: A familiar is an animal who acts like a pet for a wizard—only a familiar is much more than a pet. They have a deep connection with their wizard, and can help them with tasks from the mundane to the magical.

HIGH WIZARD: If a wizard is so practiced at their art that they can teach others, they become a high wizard. This is a high honor, for though many wizards are good at casting spells, it takes a special kind of wizard to teach magic to apprentices. All the teachers at Aldwyns are high wizards.

HOMUNCULUS: A homunculus is a creature created through a combination of magic and enchanted clay. While not actually living, they reflect the personality of the wizard who made them. They make good messengers, note-takers, and paperweights.

RUNES: Runes are part of an ancient language, created by wizards, in which each character represents a whole word. Each rune was crafted specifically—after what sometimes amounted to decades of research—to hold a particular element of magic. It is very important to draw each line of each spell's rune exactly right— otherwise the magic will at best fail. At worst, the magic will have an entirely unexpected effect.

SPELL COMPONENT: Everything from a spider's web to sand to a piece of fleece, a spell component is an object required to cast a specific spell and is used in a very specific way during the casting of the spell. A spell component is used up after one casting most of the time, but sometimes you can use the same component for multiple spells.

UNDERWIZARD: During your last year at Aldwyns, you will have a chance to become an underwizard for a high wizard. This is an opportunity for you to put your magical skills into use under the eye of an experienced wizard. After a year as an underwizard, almost all underwizards graduate Aldwyns and become wizards.

WANDWORK: All the waving and pointing wizards do with their wands is not done just for show—it is the wizards describing the parameters of the spells they want to cast. There is an art to wandwork, and the more expressive and precise the wizard's wand is, the better the spells.

WIZARD: Wizards are your standard users of magic. No longer underwizards, they fulfill vital roles in wizard society like wandmaking, potion brewing, and taking care of magical creatures.

A Wizard's Spells

Magic has a language all of its own, and in order to cast spells, wizards must learn to read and write in that mystical language. Sometimes, wizards memorize the spells and recite the necessary words from memory. Other times, however, wizards write the spells down—and then all they need to do is read them off the parchment.

Using a scroll is far easier than casting a spell from memory, but it requires preparation. You can't just write spells on any old paper with any old ink. When you write the spell, you have to infuse it with the magic of the spell itself, and the paper and ink you use have to be strong enough to hold the magic of your spell. Otherwise, all the magic you pour into the paper will bleed right out.

Unfortunately, both written spells and memorized spells are single use only. After you speak the words of a spell, the words disappear off the paper or out of your mind. You will have to memorize or write the spell down all over again.

The sensation is a bit like tickling.

Memorization

When wizards talk about having a spell memorized, it doesn't just mean that they remember the words. It means they've repeated the spell in their head over and over again until something clicks, and then they call it "memorized." There's a particular feeling associated with having a spell memorized. Many wizards describe it as feeling "like the words were burned into my mind."

Spellwriting Equipment

Fine Parchment

You must use the correct kind of paper when writing a spell. If the paper is too thin, a spell will burn right through it. Parchment is perfect for spells. It takes a long time to learn how to draw runes correctly, so you will want to practice on normal paper.

Parchment is a sheet of leather so thin you can nearly see through it.

Enchanted Rowanwood Ink

Rowan trees have natural magical properties, but it's not until you enchant the ink prepared from the sap of a rowan tree that its magical properties are fully expressed. Properly enchanted rowanwood ink is black but glitters deep gold-red in the light. If your spell takes when writing with enchanted rowanwood ink, the words will seem to burn into the paper. Enchanted rowanwood ink is expensive, though, so be sure to practice with normal ink.

that's one of the long wing feathers

Magic Quill

A magic quill is a hollow pinion from a magical bird, whose end has been cut and sharpened so that when you dip it into ink, you can write with it. Depending on the spell, you may want different kinds of feathers—a good wizard has a small collection of magic quills. For example, while phoenix feather quills are good for destruction spells, griffon feather quills are much better for writing change spells.

Spellwriting

Wizards record spells using a special vocabulary known as runes. These symbols are actually the written form of the language of magic, spoken when a wizard casts a spell. You can prepare a spell ahead of time by writing your chosen spell on a magical scroll in runes, using enchanted ink and a magic quill. To use the scroll, you have only to open it and read the runes aloud. The spell will then be released from the scroll—erasing the runes drawn on the paper. A firm foundation in basic runes is essential if you want to be a great wizard someday.

Writing a spell is much like writing a sentence. There are three runes in a basic spell. The first rune tells you what type of magic the spell falls under. The second rune tells you the intent of the spell: to harm, help, bind, or free. And the third rune—the most exciting rune—tells you the spell's effect. There are only eight choices for the first rune—one for each type of magic. There are even fewer choices for the second rune—only four! There are hundreds of options for the third rune, however. Most of your classes in spellwriting at school will be learning the options for the last rune.

A scroll is an excellent way to increase the number of spells you can cast in a given day, as most wizards can only memorize so many spells at a time (though of course, magical scrolls can only be used by a wizard who can read the runes of the spell properly).

Basic Runes

Here are the basic runes you will have to memorize in your first year. One of the first spells you will learn to write is the summon monster spell. The first rune says the spell is a summoning spell. The second rune says its intent is to bind. The third rune says the effect will be on a creature.

Example:

Ψ 中 ҙ = Summon Monster

Type + Intent + Effect = Spell

Types of Wizardry Runes

૬ Illusion

This rune means the spell will create the image of something. For example, if you wanted to create the image of fire—but not real fire, you would use this rune.

TUM-cee

ঽ Destruction

This rune means the spell will destroy something. For example, if you wanted to destroy the lock on a door, you would use this rune.

Zee-AST

Ⴤ Enchantment

This rune means the spell will be used to make someone do something. For example, if you wanted to make someone fall asleep, you would use this rune.

AHN-qua

Ψ Summoning

This rune means the spell will create something. For example, if you wanted to create an apple for a teacher, you would use this rune.

VEE-aye

ৡ Information

This rune means the spell will be used to answer a question. For example, if you wanted to find out where you had left your homework, you would use this rune.

EN-mar

ৡ Change

This rune means the spell will change a thing into something else. For example, if you wanted to turn a book into a bird, you would use this rune.

SEE-ro

Ψ Protection

This rune means the spell will protect someone. For example, if you had to walk through a storm but didn't want to get wet, you would use this rune.

YOU-et

⊌ Death

Not all death magic spells are evil—for example, if you wanted to talk to a ghost, you would use this rune.

EE-vik

Intent Runes

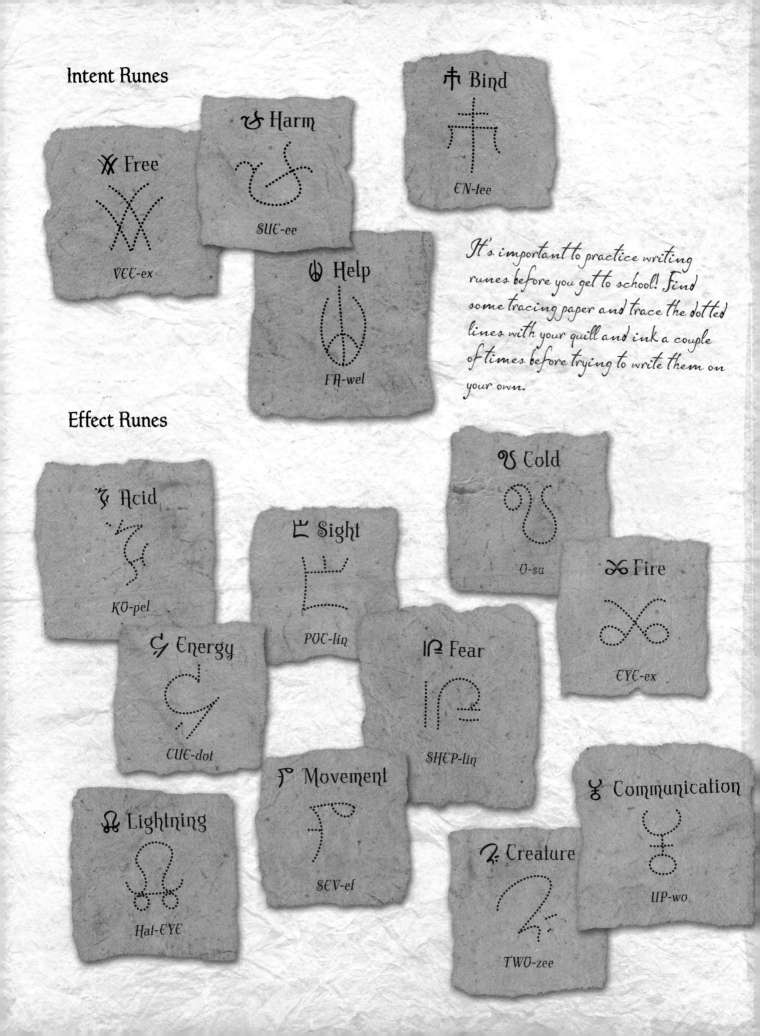

Free
VEE-ex

Harm
SUE-ee

Bind
EN-tee

Help
FA-wel

It's important to practice writing runes before you get to school! Find some tracing paper and trace the dotted lines with your quill and ink a couple of times before trying to write them on your own.

Effect Runes

Acid
KO-pel

Sight
POC-lin

Cold
O-su

Fire
EYE-ex

Energy
CUE-dot

Fear
SHEP-lin

Movement
SEV-ef

Communication
UP-wo

Lightning
Hal-EYE

Creature
TWO-zee

Wandwork

Wizards write their spells down with runes and read those runes aloud to cast spells. But they need their magic wands to set the size, duration, and location of their spells. For example, if you were going to cast a small fire spell, you would use the runes *destruction*, *free*, and *fire*, which make a spell that creates fire. But in order for the spell to work, you also need to express how big the fire will be and where you want the fire to appear. That's where wand gestures come in.

There are wand gestures for every variation of the basic spells, but here are just a few of the most important to practice before you arrive at Aldywns.

WARNING

If you forget your gestures or perform them improperly, at best nothing will happen. At worst, the spell will go off without limitations. It will be as big as your power will allow, and drain you to exhaustion! It can take days to recover from such an uncontrolled spell.

Sign: Target Self

Meaning: This gesture means your spell will affect yourself.

Description: Start by holding your wand in your right hand, pointed straight up at the sky. Move your wand to tap yourself on the head.

Sign: Not

Meaning: This gesture changes the meaning of the runes of a spell to their opposite. In addition, if you cast a spell with this sign in front of it at the same time someone else is casting the same spell without this sign, you can cause their spell to fail!

Description: Holding your wand in your right hand, move the tip of the wand from your left shoulder to your right hip.

Starting at your upper right shoulder, that's left to right!

Sign: Size

Meaning: This gesture sets the size and duration of the spell. Will it cause a big fire or a small fire? Will you summon a big spider or a small spider?

Description: Holding your wand in your right hand, draw a circle in the air counterclockwise as big as you want the spell to be powerful.

Sign: Target Other

Meaning: This gesture means that your spell will affect whatever your hands end up pointing at.

Description: Start by holding your wand in your right hand, pointed straight up at the sky. Point your wand at whatever you want to affect with your spell.

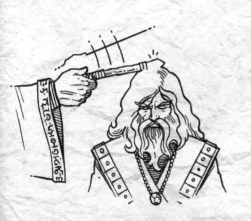

Sign: Touch

Meaning: This gesture means your spell will affect the next thing you touch other than yourself.

Description: Start by holding your wand in your right hand, pointed straight up at the sky. Move your wand to tap the head of whomever you wish to affect with the spell.

Grand Wizardry Games

During the first week of school, before the Festival of Choosing, Aldwyns hosts the Grand Wizardry Games. The games offer new students an exciting taste of each of the different arts. Some of the most anticipated games each year include the following:

Ultimate Flying Disc Competition

Students love playing Ultimate Flying Disc in our courtyard—a game composed of two teams of students operating under fly spells, trying to get the airborne disc into the other team's goal. At the Grand Wizardry Games, however, the Ultimate Flying Disc Competition is a chance for students to demonstrate their skills at Aldwyns' favorite game and to form new teams for the coming school year.

Students participating in the Ultimate Flying Disc competition wear robes that correspond to the professor who coaches their team.

The Great Treasure Hunt

Every year, Aldwyns purchases a grand prize for the Great Treasure Hunt. The professor of information magic works on a series of clever riddles that the other professors place strategically around Aldwyns to lead students to the prize. First-year students are encouraged to participate, as the Great Treasure Hunt is a great way to get to know your new school.

Last year it was a crown of animal friendship

Splatter Ball

In preparation for Splatter Ball, professors imbue five hundred water balloons with the spell Faerie Fire. When one of those water balloons hits a student, the student is both covered in water and begins to glow a bright purple. Only students who have been hit by water balloons can throw water balloons. Before the game, the previous year's Splatter Ball winner is ceremonially drenched with a water balloon. That student—the only one who can throw water balloons so far—starts the game. The last one left standing (and not glowing) wins!

Wizardry Duels

The most anticipated event of the games are the Wizardry Duels, in which wizards display their magical powers at their most potent (under the protective spells and eyes of arbitrators so that no one gets hurt).

To challenge someone to a duel at the Grand Wizardry Games, a wizardry student presents a challenge token to their opponent. This token is usually a gem of some kind, enchanted so that when the challenged person touches the stone, it will speak in the challenger's voice. The stone will continue to issue the challenge until the opponent either formally accepts or refuses the challenge. The arbitrator for the Wizardry Duels will then issue a proclamation regarding the time and place of the duel.

First-year students are prohibited from participating in the duels, though they are encouraged to attend as audience members.

Done by touching their wand to the stone, and telling it their answer.

Challenge tokens come in a variety of colors, and wizards often choose a challenge token to suit their personal colors, or the colors of their magic specialty.

WARNING

Duels are not laughing matters. Even with all the protections Aldwyns' best arbitrators afford, duels are still dangerous and risky prospects. All but first years are allowed to compete due to their training in how to use spells, and how to use spells safely. There is an optional class on dueling for those thinking of going into positions where dueling is almost expected (arbitrators, adventuring, etc.) or for those who simply wish to perform well in the senior exams.

DUELING PROCEDURE

1. The arbitrator draws a circle of thirty feet in salt.

2. Dueling wizards meet in the center of the circle, with their seconds alongside.

3. The seconds hold the wands so that they lie across both of their palms.

4. Wizards brush up the sleeves of both arms of their robes to show they are not hiding anything. The arbitrator examines both wands and wizards to ensure there is no foul play.

5. Wizards claim wands from their seconds.

6. Wizards raise wands and salute their opponents.

7. Wizards turn and walk thirteen paces.

8. The arbitrator counts to three.

9. On three, wizards turn and begin casting!

10. When the sandglass is completely empty, the arbitrator will stop both wizards and declare the winner. Wizards win points for the different spells they employ, and the wizard with the most points at the end of one sandglass's time wins.

Arbitrators oversee all duels at the Grand Wizardry Games. It is against the law for school-aged wizards to duel outside of the games.

Wizardry Etiquette

Aldwyns is your introduction to the world of wizardry, and as your guides, we make very sure all of our students come away with a firm understanding of the basic rules and regulations that govern the greater society of wizards. Magic is a huge responsibility! Just because you can cast a spell, it doesn't mean you should.

These rules help keep everyone safe. You are expected to follow these rules starting your first day of school—ignorance is no excuse. Read the list carefully, and we will look forward to meeting you on your first day of school at Aldwyns Academy!

NEVER

1. Use death magic. It is a banned art for a reason. Dabbling in this forbidden art will get you expelled.

2. Use magic to cheat on tests or disobey other school rules. Just because you can see into the future, it doesn't mean you should use that ability to cheat on your exams.

3. Use a fireball when a sleep spell will do. The spells you learn are very powerful, and if you use them to hurt others in anything other than self-defense, your wand will be taken from you until you can demonstrate the proper respect.

4. Use magic to force people to do things they wouldn't normally do. It doesn't matter if you use fists or magic. It's still bullying, and it's still forbidden.

5. Cast spells or create potions outside of the classroom. You will have to cast spells to practice your art–but that is under the practiced eye of a teacher. Accidents happen when students try out new spells outside of the classroom.

ALWAYS

1. Help other wizards in need. You're part of the great wizard family—to leave a wizard in peril is to turn your back on your family.

2. Exercise the ethical gathering of spell components. It is better to turn in an incomplete school project than to hurt a magical creature to get a missing component.

3. Share any magical discoveries with your teachers. Sometimes you've discovered something new, but sometimes those new things are dangerous and require someone with experience to handle them.

4. Be mindful of the impact your spells have on the environment around you. The spells you will learn are very powerful and need to be treated with respect and care.

5. Ask a teacher's permission before teaching magic to a non-student. Magic is a powerful tool, and we seriously weigh the qualifications of each applicant before extending them the invitation to learn magic.

Text by
Susan J. Morris

Edited by
Nina Hess

Cover art by
Eva Widermann

Interior art by
*Wayne England, Emily Fiegenschuh, David Martin,
Jim Nelson, Shane Nitzsche, Vinod Rams, Wayne Reynolds,
Joel Thomas, Beth Trott, Franz Vohwinkel, Eva Widermann*

Cartography by
Shane Nitzsche

Art Direction by
Kate Irwin

Graphic Design by
Lisa Hanson

Don't miss these other books in the Practical Guide family:

Visit our web site at **www.mirrorstonebooks.com**

A Practical Guide to Wizardry
©2008 Wizards.

Published by Wizards of the Coast, Inc. MIRRORSTONE and its logo are trademarks of Wizards of the Coast, Inc., in the U.S.A. and other countries.

Library of Congress Cataloging-in-Publication Data
A practical guide to wizardry / compiled by Arch Mage Lowadar.
  p. cm.
  ISBN 978-0-7869-5042-3
  1. Magic--Juvenile literature. 2. Wizards--Juvenile literature.
  BF1611.P73 2008
  133.4'3--dc22
                        2008001279

Printed in the U.S.A.
First Printing: August 2008
9 8 7 6 5 4 3 2 1

U.S., CANADA, ASIA, PACIFIC,
& LATIN AMERICA
Wizards of the Coast, Inc.
P.O. Box 707
Renton, WA 98057-0707
+1-800-324-6496

EUROPEAN HEADQUARTERS
Hasbro UK Ltd
Caswell Way
Newport, Gwent NP9 0YH
GREAT BRITAIN
Please keep this address for your records.

620-21941720-001-EN